Me and Meow

Adam Gudeon

me

meow

HARPER
An Imprint of HarperCollinsPublishers

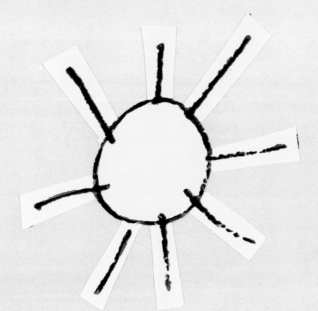

Good morning, Me!

Good morning, Meow!

Breakfast Time

Yum, Me.   Yum, Meow.

Go, Me.   Go, Meow.

Stump jumping.

Leaf leaping.

Slip sliding.

Hide hiding.

Where's Meow?

I will find my Meow.

Meow?

Meow??

I will find my Me . . .

. . . ow!

Meow!

Lunch Munching

Yum, Me.　　　Yum, Meow.

Nap Time

Wake Waking

Me, Me, Me!

Meow, Meow, Meow.

Block building.

Block knocking.

Dress-up.

Where am I?

Fine dining.

Dish washing.

Storytelling.

Bath Time

Moon dancing.

Stargazing.

Dream Dreaming

Night night, Me.

Night night, Meow.

For Monica, the cat's meow

Me and Meow

Copyright © 2011 by Adam Gudeon

All rights reserved. Manufactured in China.

No part of this book may be used or reproduced in any manner whatsoever without written permission

except in the case of brief quotations embodied in critical articles and reviews. For information address

HarperCollins Children's Books, a division of HarperCollins Publishers, 10 East 53rd Street, New York, NY 10022.

www.harpercollinschildrens.com

Library of Congress Cataloging-in-Publication Data

Gudeon, Adam.

Me and Meow / Adam Gudeon. — 1st ed.

p.   cm.

Summary: A little girl and her cat enjoy a full day of playing together.

ISBN 978-0-06-199821-8 (trade bdg.)

[1. Cats—Fiction.   2. Play—Fiction.]   I. Title.

PZ7.G93495Me 2011   2010003095

[E]—dc22   CIP

                                                                                                    AC

Typography by Martha Rago

11 12 13 14 15   SCP   10 9 8 7 6 5 4 3 2 1

❖

First Edition